The GIRL in the WINDOW

The GIRL in the WINDOW

WILMA YEO

AN
APPLE
PAPERBACK

SCHOLASTIC INC.
New York Toronto London Auckland Sydney

ISBN 0-590-43153-6

12 11 10 9 8 7 6   2 3 4/9

Printed in the U.S.A.   40

For the Smiths at Port Duncan,
where the story began, and for their children,
Jill, Jeff, Leslie, and Laura.

1

Things like kidnappings just don't happen in Meander. I mean they never had up until little Leedie Ann Alcott disappeared last summer just before my ninth birthday.

The kidnapping hit me, Kiley Mulligan Culver, a lot harder than it did the town kids because Dad and I live out on what is left of the old Alcott plantation. Losing Leedie Ann was like losing someone in my own family. In a way she was like part of my family.

Dad and I live in what was, a long, long time ago, the plantation overseer's little stone house behind the Alcott's big old mansion. My mom died when I was a baby, so as long as I can remember it's been just Dad and me.

Living out here I saw a lot of Leedie Ann, of

course. She had cute skinny braids that stuck out on each side of her head. She called me "Kiwee" which was the best she could say Kiley.

One day soon after Dad and I moved out here, Mrs. Alcott had to make a quick run to her children's clothes shop in town. She asked me to come inside the big house to babysit. When I got there Leedie Ann was still taking her nap. It was the first time I'd been inside the Alcott mansion.

The furniture was dark and heavy and as polished as a pond on a still day. The house was so quiet that when the refrigerator clicked on I about jumped out of my chair. Leedie woke up soon after that, which I was glad of. We played, and I made her a doll out of a clothespin and some scraps from her kiddie sewing basket.

After that she'd tag around the place after me whenever I went down to visit the kennel dogs or when I went to the end of the lane to get our mail. Even though I never went inside the Alcott mansion again, I saw a lot of Leedie Ann. I got so I really cared about that quiet little kid. Sometimes I even pretended she was my very own little sister.

She was only four when it happened. The day she disappeared our whole town turned into a giant search party. I guess no one in Meander, least of all me, will ever forget that day in late summer.

It was hotter than today. Funny how you remember little things about a day when something earth-shaking happened.

I remember that as I rode my bike past the piney woods coming home from school that afternoon, a family of pelicans rose from behind the trees. They were on their way, as always this time of day, to the ocean to catch fish then fly home and share the food with their young.

Only instead of flying in formation behind one leader as usual, there were two birds at the head of the line. The line was all out of kilter as if the floppy giant birds were confused or scared.

Their great fringe-tipped wings beat frantically at the heavy air. I thought for the first time how scary these birds looked.

Before I got all the way up our lane Dad came running down to meet me! Half his shirttail was flapping, his arms were outspread, and his hair was hanging like short bangs over his forehead.

3

For a dreadful split second I felt as if Dad had turned into a giant pelican flapping awkwardly toward me.

"Kiley Mulligan! Thank God you're safe," he shouted before we even met.

I braked my bike and dropped one foot to the ground, waiting speechless because of Dad's strange actions. My dad used to be a high school English literature teacher. He still looks like one even though he's on leave to write a book.

He grabbed hold of my handlebar, and I could feel him shaking right through my rubber grips. "Have you seen Leedie Ann?" he demanded, as if I was responsible for her.

Still speechless, I shook my head, which by then was buzzing like it was full of swamp mosquitos.

"She's gone," Dad said, letting go of my bike.

"Gone where?" I asked. Then I realized how dumb that was. If he knew he wouldn't be acting this way.

Dad's hands hung limp at his sides. "The school bus driver let Leedie Ann off at her own door at two. Mrs. Alcott had car trouble on her way home. She was late getting there. When she did, Leedie was gone. She *had* been home because her toy sewing basket was scattered over the kitchen floor."

"But maybe she just wandered — off?" I said. I was shaking now, too. Leedie Ann gone? Alone? But she was so little.

Dad looked over toward the marsh where the saw grasses and the sweet grasses grew knee high. "We've searched the woods. She wouldn't go near the ocean, or the swamp, because she knows about alligators. She's not on the road, nor the marsh, nor in the old slave quarters." He turned and started back up the lane.

I walked my bike along behind him. "Once Clara Mae McLean's little brother was lost and they found him asleep in his own bed," I called ahead to Dad. I couldn't — I didn't *want* to believe that something bad had happened to little Leedie.

Dad didn't even answer — just shook his head. "Half the police force searched the Alcott house and grounds," he said. "They found strange tire tracks — skid marks — in the back drive. That's all."

Dad made me stay around close to home all the rest of the day.

The whole thing was unreal and scary. If Leedie Ann, a real, little person, with one dimple and

skinny braids, could disappear, then anyone could
— anything could happen.

The search parties hunted day and night. Leedie Ann's father, who is divorced from her mother
and lives in a different state, came to help. Then
the FBI agents came.

Almost everyone in town was questioned. The
first person the agents talked to was Mr. Alcott
himself. They even had his house searched, I heard,
but they didn't find a trace of Leedie Ann.

A teenage boy from Blessville, out on parole
from stealing cars, was questioned. And old George
Bender was brought up from his shack on Undertow Beach to the police station for questioning.
They even talked to Old Terry, who comes to take
care of the kennel dogs, although everyone knew
he wouldn't harm a flea. But after a while everyone drifted back to his own place.

Even though there was never a ransom note,
people in Meander were sure Leedie Ann was
kidnapped and not just lost. Finally people stopped
talking about it, but nobody forgot.

2

Everything changed after Leedie disappeared. The very next day a Gypsy woman walked up to the back door of the Alcott house and knocked. The door opened and the woman vanished inside.

Late summer is the time of year the Gypsies come to our part of the country because winters are warm here. We're used to seeing their caravans. Everyone knows they camp until spring in the woods back of Undertow Beach, but they don't usually come right up to the houses in Meander.

The Gypsy woman stayed on with Mrs. Alcott and after that I would see her walking down our lane to pick up the mail. Her black hair hung to her shoulders. Her skin was dark and wrinkled. Sometimes she wore an orange beret dipped in front by a bangle of heavy purple beads. There was something exciting and almost mysterious about her.

We knew her name was Pesha because every so often there was a letter addressed "Pesha" in the mailbox down by Crescent Cross Road that we shared with Alcotts. That's all — just Pesha. I looked, but there was never any stamp or return address.

Pretty soon I got used to seeing Pesha walking down for their mail. I'd wave and even say hello to her. It was lonely out here with Leedie Ann gone. Pesha and Old Terry might be the only people besides Dad I'd see if it wasn't a school day. Though Pesha would always wave at me, there was something secretive and forbidding about the way she looked and acted.

The people around Meander didn't see Mrs. Alcott much after the kidnapping, either. She closed her children's clothes shop in town. My friend Sarah's mother said she thought it was strange of Mrs. Alcott to take up with a Gypsy. But Pesha stayed on, even though spring came and the other Gypsies left.

It was a mystery, all right. Nobody knew anything until about two weeks ago, when the really exciting things started to happen. And I was right in the middle of it all.

That night, two weeks ago, I was cutting through the back way to our house after telling the kennel dogs good night. It was new dark and so quiet I could hear the ocean sighing in its bed. As I passed the big house I looked up at the second floor.

"Leedie!" I yelled so loud that I set off the kennel dogs way down by the old slave quarters.

I yelled because there, looking out the window of her very own room, stood Leedie Ann herself! I was shocked to the spot. Leedie just stood staring out into the night while the kennel dogs' barking turned into worried whimpers, and from the swamps beyond I could hear the whippoorwill's wailing.

Suddenly I saw a shadowy figure swoop across the bedroom and yank the window curtain closed. That set me free. I ran fast as I could to tell Dad.

Dad was hanging up his favorite old tweed jacket and missed the hook as I burst through the screen door with my exciting news. I was so happy I was laughing and crying at the same time. "Leedie's home!" I cried even before the screen door slammed behind me.

Dad heard me out before he stooped to pick up his jacket. "Not so, Kiley Mulligan," he said. "You saw a shadow of some kind and that poor little kid is still on your mind. You've got to stop imagining things. First thing you know nobody will believe a word you say."

"But Dad," I almost yelled, "I saw her. Her mom, or someone, was in the room, too. I saw them both. Just go ask!"

"What you are saying does not make sense," Dad said sternly.

My news was bursting inside me. I felt desperate. How could I make him understand this had really happened? I tried sounding hurt. "You never believe me!"

"Don't you see," Dad argued, "the sheriff would have been notified. The firehouse siren would have gone off. Everyone in Meander would know."

I looked him straight in the eye. "I know what I saw, and I saw Leedie Ann," I said, emphasizing each word.

I could feel my face all screwed up from being frustrated. I was so sure I was right that my nose itched. "If you don't go over I'll — I'll go myself,"

I said. Somebody had to do something.

Dad tightened his lips, and I could almost see all my past mistakes clicking through his mind like on an adding machine. At last he took a deep breath and said, "I suppose I could just go to the door and ask if Mrs. Alcott needs anything. She has shut herself in ever since this happened — her and that Gypsy woman holding seances." He seemed almost to be talking to himself now — like he'd forgotten I was even there. But he was putting on his jacket so I knew I had him pretty much convinced.

"You'll see!" I said, still so happy I couldn't stand still.

Dad started for the door, then stopped. "If what you are saying is not true, going over there could be a bad mistake," he said.

"It's true," I said on a hiccup because the excitement of seeing Leedie was making bubbles inside me. I whispered it again. "It's true."

I watched Dad go out the door. Now you'll see, I thought. He disappeared right away into the shadows. Everything was quiet except for the swamp singing its night song.

Why hadn't Mrs. Alcott told the whole world that Leedie was home? Did it have anything to do with Pesha, the Gypsy woman?

My friend Sarah's mother is afraid of Gypsies. She says that when Pesha holds seances she calls down spirits of the dead. She says these spirits can put spells on people. Had Pesha put a spell on Mrs. Alcott?

When I was a little kid I heard someone say that Mrs. Alcott had "old money." I imagined piles of worn-smooth silver and wrinkled-soft paper money. But now I know it means her money was left to her when her folks died, the same as the house and land were left to Leedie Ann's father by his folks.

So some day the money would go to Leedie Ann — if they ever found her. And now I was sure they had. I'd never been more sure of anything.

In just a little while, I promised myself as I waited for Dad to come back, the siren will go off. Maybe we would even be able to hear the town people cheering from out here. But even though I had seen Leedie myself, inside I had a creepy feeling like a swamp snake had crawled down the back of my shirt. "She's there," I whispered out into the darkness. "I saw her!"

A few minutes later Dad's shadowy figure appeared on the narrow sandy path to our door. I could tell by the slow way he walked he had not heard good news. But with Leedie safely back home, what other news could he have heard?

"Mrs. Alcott didn't say anything about Leedie," Dad said as soon as he was inside. He dropped into his leather chair. "She'd have told me, of course. Dear God, that woman has aged in one year." Dad rubbed his chin and looked at me as if he was trying to decide whether to lecture me or disown me.

I turned away and walked over to the window that faces the dimly lit back portico of the Alcott house. I stared again into the shadows. Something strange was going on inside that house — I was sure of that. Could that Gypsy woman have something to do with it? I felt tears coming, but I choked them back.

3

I didn't say anything more about Leedie Ann to Dad. I had already lost enough points with him. When my friend Sarah's dad can't understand *her*, Sarah's mother explains how Sarah feels. I couldn't remember my mother. If she were alive would she understand how mixed up I felt about all this?

I tried to tell myself my imagination had run away with me again, like Dad said. But I knew that wasn't true. I *had* seen Leedie Ann right there in her own bedroom window!

There was only one way to prove Leedie Ann truly was back home. It would be risky. And I'd need help. I was almost sure I could depend on Sarah, my best friend, to help me.

A great plan was beginning to act itself out in my mind. Sarah always complains that my wild plans get her into trouble. But she always goes along with them. I was doubly sure she would this time, no matter how dangerous it was. Right this minute inside her own house, Leedie Ann, and maybe Mrs. Alcott, too, were surely in trouble. All I had to do was convince Sarah that I really had seen Leedie with my very own eyes.

I always go by for Sarah on school days. Since the Alcott plantation is about two miles out from Meander, I bike as far as Sarah's house. Then I stash my bike in their carport and we walk the rest of the way to school together.

The morning after I saw Leedie Ann in the window, I set out a little early so Sarah and I would have time to talk. There was a stiff breeze off oceanside flattening the sweet marsh grass. The soft air smelled salty and a little like dead fish.

I hadn't been able to get Leedie off my mind all night long. It was like she was calling out to me for help.

I could almost hear her pitiful little voice in the wind as I rode down the long lane leading out from our place, then turned on to Crescent Cross Road.

15

Crescent Cross Road is black-topped and winds a couple of miles through the piney woods and past the swamps into town.

Sarah's family was still at the breakfast table. I didn't want to say anything in front of her mom and dad or her brother, Adam. Adam's fifteen. Sarah's mother is sort of what you might call protective of her. I didn't want her to imagine I was going to get Sarah mixed up in anything dangerous.

But my news was like a big drum beating inside me, and Sarah's mom noticed. "You look feverish, Kiley," she said. "Feel okay? There isn't anything wrong, is there?" Other kids' mothers sometimes look at me the way she was now. Sort of worried that maybe I was contagious. Especially Sarah's mother.

"No, nothing's wrong," I said real quick. "And no fever. I guess it's the fresh air."

"Air's fresh every morning, Riley," Sarah's brother Adam said, without looking up from his eggs. He always calls me Riley instead of Kiley, but I don't mind.

Usually I would have laughed the way I knew

Adam wanted me to — just to make a good impression on him. But today I was too eager to get Sarah out of there.

She seemed slower than usual. Sarah has a way of making every move look important. At last she folded her napkin — they use cloth ones at every meal — and stacked her silverware on her plate to carry to the counter. That's one of the rules her mom has. She has lots.

Soon as we were outside I told Sarah my exciting news. I finished up with, ". . . and there she stood! Right in the window big as life — big as any four-year-old. Well, almost five now."

Sarah grabbed me by the shoulders. "Kiley," she cried, "didn't you tell your father?" Even with braces and her mouth dropped open Sarah is pretty. In fact her braces make her look more interesting in a cared-for sort of way.

"Of course I told my dad," I said. Then I told her about that part of it. "Mrs. Alcott is real strange now," I went on. "She doesn't like anyone bothering her. Even Dad says she'll hardly talk to him. We just get a glimpse of her now and then as she drives over to the country store for food."

17

"My mother says it's a wonder Mrs. Alcott hasn't lost her mind," Sarah said. "Living there with that Gypsy and all."

"You can see why Dad doesn't believe me," I said. "I swear, Sarah, there is something really spooky going on in the big house. That's why you are going to have to be real brave to help with my plan."

"What plan?" Sarah looked suspicious already.

"We have to get inside that house," I said.

"We?"

"And we have to do it right away. Or rather you do," I said.

"Absolutely not!" Sarah stopped right in the middle of the sidewalk.

I used my most pleading voice. "Will you just listen?" I looked Sarah straight in the eye. "We have to carry out my plan right away. Tomorrow morning, in fact. It's like your mom says; Pesha must have cast a spell on Mrs. Alcott. Why else wouldn't she tell Dad that Leedie is home? Don't worry. My plan is foolproof."

"Like the time we set our garage on fire trying to hatch baby birds — "

"Sarah!" I interrupted, "Leedie Ann is a lot

more important than baby birds. All you have to do is get inside the big house and make sure and positive I saw Leedie."

"All!"

"From then on I'll take over."

"Why don't *you* go in?"

"Because my plan won't work if it's me."

"Why not?" Sarah demanded.

"Because I've been in that house before. Mrs. Alcott knows that I know there is a bathroom downstairs and — "

"Kiley Mulligan, I don't see — "

"Look," I interrupted, shrugging to show her there was nothing to it, "you simply take off up the stairway before Mrs. Alcott or Pesha has a chance to say there is a bathroom downstairs you can use."

"*Bathroom?*" Sarah stopped walking and backed up a couple of steps as if I was going to push her inside the Alcott house right then and there.

Other kids on their way to school, too, were beginning to turn and stare back at Sarah and me after they passed by us. I waited until no one was in earshot and said, "Let me explain. Tomorrow is Saturday. Soon as Dad leaves for town to get groceries, I'll leave, too. But I'll only go to the end of our lane. You ride your bike out Crescent Cross Road and meet me. I'll hide out there at the end of the lane while you go on up to the big house."

We were getting pretty close to school now. Sarah was walking faster and faster as if she was trying to escape.

I took hold of her arm to slow her down and finished up all in one breath, "You ride straight up the lane to my house. You knock, and of course, there won't be anyone home, so go on across to Mrs. Alcott's back door and say you have to use a bathroom quick and that I'm not home. Then when you get inside, dash off up the staircase. See?" I pleaded.

Sarah sighed like she does when she's about to give in to one of my plans — which she never likes right off but does get used to. "I knew you would," I said real quick before she could change her mind. "You can see this is a plan that can't fail. And it's safe."

"Safe? In that big spooky house? With that Pesha Gypsy in there? And Mrs. Alcott maybe gone crazy from worry?" She shook her head and shifted her books to her other arm. There wasn't time to say more because we'd reached school.

I noticed that Sarah was looking around at the other kids going in like she was trying to choose someone else for a best friend. So I added one last clincher. "We'll be the heroes of Meander by tomorrow night," I promised in a whisper.

"Yes, or dead," Sarah muttered. But I knew she had given in for sure.

4

The first thing I thought of the next morning was Leedie Ann. At breakfast I was so nervous that something would go wrong with my plan that I kept dropping things. After I had made my second mess Dad complained that he was already six pages behind schedule on the book he was working on, and would I please be more careful.

I was so afraid he might put off his regular Saturday morning trip to town that I said, "Ha-ha, six little pages — that's nothing."

Now Dad knew that I knew that six pages behind could turn him from a loving father into a raving maniac. He looked at me suspiciously. "What are you up to now, Kiley Mulligan?" he asked.

I felt this stupid grin come on my face which I was sure made things look all the worse. I shrugged and tried to look casual. "Nothing," I said. "Sarah's coming out and we'll just mess around."

"Looks to me like you've already done that," Dad said as I wiped up the cup of cocoa I'd spilled.

To my relief Dad left a little earlier than usual. But, I reminded myself, that also means he'll be back earlier, too. As soon as his pickup truck was out of sight, I hopped on my bike and headed out as if I was leaving, too — just in case someone in the big house was watching.

At the end of our sandy lane there is a big clump of yaupon bushes. I wrestled my bike out of sight in the bushes and hunkered down in the deep saw grass to wait for Sarah to arrive as we planned.

Just when I thought she must have backed out, I saw her bike turning off Crescent Cross Road onto our lane.

The coast was clear, so I stood up and silently signaled Sarah on. I could tell by the way her bike wobbled and weaved slowly up our lane that her heart was not in this rescue operation. But right that minute there was nothing I could do except stay hidden in that scratchy grass and count on her following my instructions.

The next wait dragged on forever. My nose tingled from the tickle of yaupon leaves which smelled sickeningly like hot tea. Something bit me under my jeans. The bite was in the sweaty bend of my knee just out of reach for scratching.

After a while I forgot about being uncomfortable and began to worry. I pictured Sarah inside that big creepy house. I thought about the Gypsy woman's psychic powers. What if Leedie Ann never had been kidnapped? What if all this time she'd been hidden away inside that house? What if Sarah disappeared now, too, the way Leedie had?

I dug at the bite through my jeans leg and tried desperately to think of a plan to rescue Sarah. Just as I told myself I'd have to go knock on Mrs. Alcott's door myself, I heard the secret whistle Sarah and I used — two shorts and a long. I didn't even wait to see if the coast was clear. I jumped out and ran to the middle of the lane.

Sarah's face was smudged with tears. She hopped off her bike and I hugged her so hard we both almost fell backward across the bike. For some stupid reason we both started laughing and crying at the same time. But it wasn't a funny-laugh.

"Kiley! I saw her!" Sarah said, and her eyes

squinched almost closed like she was trying to shut something out.

"Swear?" I cried rubbing at the goose pimples on my arms.

"I *saw* Leedie Ann!" she repeated as if she was in a daze.

"And?" I prodded to keep her talking. She looked like she might faint instead. She was white as the sand pipers along the beaches. My own heart was pounding against my sweaty T-shirt, which felt icy across my shoulder blades.

Sarah took a sobbing breath. "It was awful!"

"What was?" I begged. "Sarah, please start at the beginning. Tell me everything." I heard a car motor. "Oh, Pete's sake, here comes my dad."

Luckily Dad just waved and drove on past. I silently thanked some angel (since I hated to bother God over such a thing as deceiving my father) that he was six pages behind and in a hurry to get home. Otherwise he might have asked what I was "up to" again.

"And Leedie. When did you see Leedie?" I whispered.

"There's worse before that," Sarah cried, shaking her wrists the way she does when she's really upset.

"Take a deep breath," I said, "but go on."

"Mrs. Alcott let me in okay," Sarah said as she let out the breath. "She had this weird look, though, like she was scared there was something behind her. I couldn't see the Gypsy woman anywhere, which gave me the creeps because I thought that might be what she was afraid of."

"You were brave," I said. "Go on."

"I ran up the stairs," Sarah said slowly, as if she was reading it from a book. "I shut and locked the bathroom door. I waited a while then flushed in case someone was listening." Sarah hiccupped. "Oh, Kiley, in that quiet house the flush sounded like an explosion! All I wanted was to get out of there."

"But you *did* see Leedie — "

Sarah nodded. Her eyes were wide. "Yes, but that was the awful part." She took another deep breath without me telling her. "When I left the bathroom I tiptoed into the hall and over to Leedie's door, which was where you said it would be."

"Pete's sake, Sarah," I almost yelled because she was so maddeningly slow.

"She was in there," Sarah said, "but I barely got a glimpse of her when someone behind me dug their fingers into my shoulder." Now tears were streaming again down Sarah's cheeks.

"Who — " I began.

For once in her life Sarah seemed in a hurry to say something. "The Gypsy!" she interrupted me.

"Sarah!" I said, mostly to myself. "Then Pesha really does have them under a spell."

"Yes!" Sarah agreed, wiping her face with a folded tissue from her skirt pocket. "She muttered something at me in this low, whispery voice. Sounded like *gorgio*. I know what it means, too, because I read this book once — "

"Sarah!" I *did* yell this time. "Who cares about a book you read. What happened next?"

"In that same low voice she said, 'You bring the evil eye! Go!' " Sarah's voice trembled as she imitated Pesha. Then Sarah went on, "I got out fast. I didn't see Mrs. Alcott again."

"But Leedie Ann was really there?" I asked.

"I swear," Sarah said, refolding the tissue and putting it back in her pocket.

"This calls for *real* action," I declared. "What we need now is a new plan."

5

While I was guiding my bike from behind the bushes, I had the perfect idea. "I've got it!" I called to Sarah who was still standing in the middle of the lane. "And you don't have to do a thing," I added quickly when I saw the look on her face.

"I wouldn't, even if you asked," Sarah said hysterically. I wanted to remind her that without me her life would be awfully dull. Sarah's idea of a good plan is "let's make peanut butter fudge."

"This will not be dangerous," I assured her. "All I need from you is — do you have any money?"

"I still have my allowance," she admitted. "Why?"

"I'll explain when we get where we can talk in

private," I said. "This has to be kept double dog dead secret."

"Kiley Mulligan, how much more privacy do you need?" Sarah cried, waving her hand to include the field of marsh grasses empty except for the ginko tree with its fan-shaped leaves dancing like tiny, green ballerinas.

"We'll need paper and pencil," I told her.

"Well, I'm not going anywhere near that house again," Sarah said, glancing darkly back up our lane. "Maybe never!"

"Anyway, Dad might overhear us at my house," I admitted. "We'll ride into town to your house. Then go up in your tree house to work out the details. Then we'll need your money to get special writing paper."

"I hate it when you act mysterious, Kiley," Sarah said. She looked close to crying again. I thought about all she'd been through that morning. I looked around to be sure we were completely alone. "Okay," I whispered. "We're going to write a letter to Pesha and put it in our mailbox for her to pick up when she gets their mail."

"Kiley!" Sarah screamed.

I clapped my hand over her mouth.

She peeled my hand away. "Maybe *you* are, but I'm not," she said. "This time, for once, I really mean it, Kiley."

I decided the best thing to do was ignore what she'd just said. She was still upset. "Try not to look so shook-up when we get to your house, Sarah," I said calmly. "Your mother notices things like that."

"Are you sure we shouldn't just tell — " Sarah began.

"Positively not!" I said. "You know how your mom feels about Gypsies. She won't let you out of the house for weeks. Anyway, you'd have to admit how you found out that Leedie is home again. First thing, we'll go up in your tree house and plan the letter. I have to think."

"The last time you thought," Sarah said grudgingly, "we both nearly drowned in the ocean."

"Yes, but we didn't drown," I reminded her. I knew what she meant. Once when Sarah and I were shelling on Undertow Beach, we saw a baby sandpiper clinging to something that was floating on top of the high waves. He looked like he had a broken wing.

The waves washed him closer, and I saw that the poor bird was tangled in a piece of yellow rope tied to a float off of a shrimp boat.

The waves would sweep him closer to shore, then he'd be pulled back again. We'd long ago learned that you don't go in the ocean at Undertow Beach, but I talked Sarah into holding my hand while I tried to get hold of the rope. The strong undertow there pulled us both under water, but when I came up I had hold of the rope and we saved the bird.

I ignored Sarah's remark. "Let's get started. We've got a lot to do." I wanted *so* much for things to hurry and get back the way they were before Leedie was kidnapped.

When we got to Sarah's house in town I sent her on inside to get a tablet and pencil so we could plan our letter to Pesha. I walked my bike around back to the huge, old live oak where the tree house is. Just to keep in practice I ignored the ladder and climbed up to the tree house on the thick wisteria vine that snakes around the big tree's trunk.

I sat cross-legged on the square of floor. I was almost hidden from below by the tree's giant limbs hung with spidery veils of gray Spanish moss. People in Meander say that Spanish moss, which I call witches' hair, only grows as far in from the ocean as you can hear the surf pound. From Sarah's tree house, at least, that is true. I sat there thinking about what to say in the letter.

In a little bit Sarah came up the ladder with the pencil and tablet.

"We have to plan this carefully," I warned her. "We want Pesha to know that the person who writes the letter knows about Leedie Ann."

Sarah leaned back on her flattened palms as if she wanted to get as far away as possible from what I was going to write.

"I'm not signing it," she warned me.

"We don't either one sign it!" I said, beginning to feel cross with her because of all her objections. "You're no help when you act like this. We want Pesha to think the letter is from the friend who writes to her sometimes. When she answers our letter we'll have solid evidence to take to the police."

"The *police*?" Sarah scooted back a few inches. "Kiley, I don't — "

"To your folks then," I said to keep Sarah from

backing right on out of the tree house. "Now let's plan what to say. Since we've got to make the letter sound like it came from another Gypsy, I wonder how they talk."

"Like I tried to tell you a while ago, Kiley," Sarah said primly, "I read this book once, and it had lots of Gypsy words in it. The girl in it, her name was — "

"Sarah!" I interrupted her. "That's great! What were the Gypsy words?" Sarah is very smart and the things she knows come in handy pretty often.

"Well," Sarah said, "their language is called Romany. One word I remember was *Dell-o-del*. Really that's three words."

"But what does it mean?" I asked.

"It means, God give you luck," she said. "We — I mean you, could sign the letter that way."

"Perfect!" I said.

So this is the way our letter read.

Pesha,
   I need to know your future plans for the little Alcott girl. Answer early Thursday morning in mail box at end of lane. Mark envelope with an X only.
                        Dell-o-del

"Now we'll need some plain paper and an envelope so nobody can trace the letter to us — just in case," I told Sarah.

We rode our bikes down to Timkins' Variety Store and bought some plain paper and short envelopes like I'd seen addressed to Pesha in our box. Outside Timkins' I took out one sheet of paper and one envelope. I dropped the rest in the Demsy Dumpster on the grocery store parking lot.

When we got back to Sarah's tree house I made a copy of our letter. I wrote "Pesha" on the envelope like I'd seen on her other letters.

"I'll be able to keep a watch for the mail carrier on Wednesday because school will be out for the summer," I explained to Sarah. "Just as soon as he leaves I'll put our letter with the rest of the mail. You see, there's nothing to it."

"I hope not," Sarah said. "If we get in trouble one more time I'm almost sure my mother will say you and I can't be friends anymore because she already said — "

"We won't," I said before she could finish. As I swung myself down the thick vine I added silently, I hope. It was true that it was always my

34

ideas that got Sarah and me into trouble. But not be Sarah's friend? I couldn't even bear to think of that.

In my heart I suspected that Sarah's mother already didn't like me much. I always figured it was because I didn't have a mother myself, and she didn't have much faith in fathers raising kids alone.

But somebody had to do something about Lee-die Ann, and maybe her mother, too — prisoners in their own house. This was the best way I knew of to find out once and for all if the Gypsy woman *was* holding them prisoner.

I told Sarah good-bye and not to worry and rode my bike off toward Crescent Cross Road and home. Real soon now, I promised myself, everything at the Alcott plantation will be back the way it used to be. Then maybe even Sarah's mom will think some of my plans are worthwhile.

6

For the rest of Saturday and all day Sunday I kept an eye on the big house. The heavy curtain at Leedie's window was still closed. Not one thing moved over there.

Old Terry came on Sunday, and I was glad of the chance to help him down at the kennel.

After that I tried to read, but the only book I had wasn't nearly as exciting as what was going on right now in my own life.

A couple of times I got the letter out from under my bed where I'd hidden it and read it again. Each time I did I got little chill bugs crawling up my backbone.

Monday and Tuesday, the last two days of school, dragged past. I couldn't get Leedie off my mind.

I even almost forgot to look at my report card

36

after Mrs. McDonald passed them out. Sarah got all A's as usual. I got an A in English. I thought about showing it to Sarah's mom to see if that would make her like me better. But I didn't because beside Sarah's report, mine would not have impressed her.

Sarah's mom has strict rules about homework. My dad just says, "Honey, if you want to learn, nothing can stop you. And if you don't want to learn, nobody can make you." My problem is that sometimes I want to and sometimes I'd rather do something else.

Wednesday morning came at last. Outside, the sky was dark and stormy-looking. The wind was blowing so hard that the long palmetto fronds outside my window sounded like a whip, crackling and popping.

I wished Sarah could come out to our house to wait with me for the mail carrier to go past. But I knew she couldn't because she and her mom had planned to drive to the city to shop.

"Hey, Kiley Mulligan," Dad said after breakfast, "how come you're not getting ready for school?"

"School's out, Dad," I reminded him. I really

didn't blame Dad for forgetting. When he's working on a new book, the higher the stack of pages, the more absent-minded he gets. He hadn't even remembered to ask about my report card yet. Anyway, I had more important things to think about myself.

I knew the mail carrier usually stopped at the end of our lane about ten o'clock. I can usually tell the sound of his jeep from the few other cars that come this far out on Crescent Cross Road.

All I had to do was be sure and slip my letter to Pesha in the box between the time the mail carrier left and when Pesha came to pick up their mail. I had on a large sweatshirt to cover the letter tucked into the top of my jeans.

Dad was hunched over his typewriter and didn't look up as I started out the front door. I sat on our front step and stared over at the big stone house. The house seemed to have swallowed up the people inside it. There used to be a young Mexican gardener who came every day, but Mrs. Alcott sent him away right after the kidnapping. Now the liana vines and bitter-berry bushes grew wild, and the wind swept shadows over the knee-deep knot grass.

It was almost ten o'clock. I couldn't sit still another second, so I decided to ride my bike slowly down the lane. In all this wind, I thought, I might even miss the sound of the mail carrier's jeep.

He was nowhere in sight when I got to Crescent Cross Road, so I dropped one foot to the ground, listening and hoping no one else would come along.

I jumped as I heard a sudden noise above the wind, but it was only the sea gulls shrieking like they do in a storm. Funny how perfectly ordinary sounds like that seem spooky when you are already jittery about something. I felt the letter to make sure it was safe.

At last I heard the sound I was listening for. I waited until I could tell the jeep was close, then turned my bike around as if I was really heading up the lane. I didn't want the carrier to get suspicious.

Soon as I heard his jeep pull away I turned around again. I had to get my letter in the box and get home before Pesha came. I sure didn't want to meet her face to face today.

I slipped my letter in with the others. Then I made a quick check to see if Dad had any mail. He didn't, so I rode on back home.

Once inside our house I guess I was sort of pacing around, trying to keep a watch for Pesha to come out. Anyway, Dad said, "Settle down, honey, you're acting like a caged monkey."

"Umm, I was just going down to see the kennel dogs," I said quickly. I didn't want Dad getting suspicious, either.

The kennel dogs are always glad to see me. Even though they have a nice big shelter house and a long run, I feel sorry for them. They used to be Mr. Alcott's hunting dogs. The dogs really have long, important-sounding names, but I've given them my own private nicknames. I call the bold one with a black spot over his eye, Pirate. I call the big one who is polite, Boss, and the shy prettiest one who has sad eyes, Violet.

From the kennels, which are a ways in front of the five little crumbly brick buildings once used as slave quarters, I could easily watch for Pesha to start down after their mail. Sure enough, in a few minutes she came out Mrs. Alcott's back door. She was dressed in a red, flowered skirt that came almost to her ankles. She had sandals on her bare brown feet. She had tied a blue kerchief around her head. I kept close watch as she darted down the lane like a small nervous bird.

I watched again when she came back up the lane and disappeared through the back door of the big house. It was a scary feeling to know she'd had my letter right there in her hand. Thinking about it made my nose tingle into a sneeze. I rubbed the chilly back of my neck. I'd really have to keep a close watch on the mailbox from now until Pesha's answer came.

But the answer to my letter was never put in the mailbox. Instead, the worst thing that could happen — did.

7

Thursday morning, the day I expected Pesha to answer our letter, Dad was in an uproar because his last typewriter cassette ran out. That meant a trip into town for more. Before he had a chance to ask me to go along, I offered to do the breakfast dishes alone.

Dad said, "Right! Thanks!" and hurried on out to his pickup.

I knew I had plenty of time to check the mailbox for Pesha's answer before the mail carrier came. Still I was hurrying so from excitement that I spilled the cereal milk and had to mop that up.

When the kitchen was back in order, I paced around the house until the hands of the clock finally crept toward ten. Then, with a quick glance toward the big house I headed my bike down our lane.

I didn't even get a fourth of the way down when Dad's pickup truck turned in off Crescent Cross Road.

He stopped alongside of me. "Come straight on back up to the house," he called through his open car window. "I don't want you wandering around." He looked excited and sort of worried.

Since Dad hardly ever worries about me, I got a cloudy mixed-up feeling in my head and in my stomach, too. I had to mind Dad. But what about Pesha's answer? Would the mail carrier leave it there?

I had barely leaned my bike against the side of our house when Dad said from the doorway, "There's news, Kiley. They've re-opened the Alcott kidnapping case. I want you to stick around close here until they find out a few more things."

"Then Leedie Ann *is* home!" I cried. "I *tried* to tell you but — "

"Kiley!" Dad's no-nonsense voice stopped me like a slap. "I told you to end that foolishness. Leedie is not home — she's still missing. But there

43

is hope again. The Gypsy woman, Pesha, has received a letter that — "

For a second it was as if I had gone blind and deaf. Dad's voice sounded far away and everything looked black. I gave my head a little shake and Dad's voice tuned back in saying, " — and Mrs. Alcott has turned the letter over to the police, of course. Pesha denies knowing anything about it, and Mrs. Alcott believes her. But the police are going to investigate."

The police! Our letter! *My* letter. The police had it! My fingerprints! Jail! Scary thoughts shot at my head like it was a target for darts.

"Don't get so upset, Kiley Mulligan." Dad's voice was softened. "The person who wrote the letter probably knows where Leedie Ann is. But even if Gypsies have Leedie, as the police suspect now, they won't harm her — nor you."

"I — I'm not scared," I said trying to breathe some air that felt like new air instead of used up.

Never in all the thinking I had done about my letter to Pesha had I ever thought it would end up with the police. "What — I mean what are they going to do? I mean the police?" My lips felt like plastic. My whole face felt stiff, as if I'd just come from swimming in the salty ocean.

"They'll take Pesha in for questioning," Dad said in a father-knows-best voice. I tried to act more normal — as if I was only curious. I was lucky Dad wasn't practically a mind reader like Sarah's mom, or he would already be suspicious of the way I was acting.

I swallowed twice and sort of brushed at my hair, trying to look just interested. "What will they do to the person — I mean the Gypsy — who wrote the letter?"

He turned to go to his desk. "All you need to be concerned about is sticking here close until things change one way or the other," he said. "Now I've got to get my mind off this and get to work."

All I needed to be concerned about! If only he knew. His own daughter was a criminal! Surely if he knew that he would forget about that book he was writing and help me.

Dad had said that the person who wrote the letter to Pesha probably knew where Leedie Ann was. Well, that much was right. I did know. She was inside the big house. Knowing that made me feel a little better.

And then I began to get mad. Mad at Mrs. Alcott for not *telling* the whole world that Leedie Ann was safe at home. Mad at Pesha in case she really *had* put a spell on Mrs. Alcott so that she couldn't tell. Most of all mad at Dad for not being a mother who I could talk to. I tried to stay mad at them all because I knew if I wasn't mad, I'd be so scared I couldn't think straight.

I need to talk to Sarah, I thought. And I need a new plan, too. But most of all, until I think of what to do, I need to tell Sarah, "No matter what happens, do *not* tell anyone that we wrote the letter!"

Dad was already shuffling papers. "I'm going down to see the kennel dogs," I told him. He looked up and said, "All right. But no farther away, you hear?"

I said okay and started out the door. All three dogs had their noses up against the wire run by the time I got there. I sat down in the long grass and started talking to them. "I was only trying to help Leedie Ann," I said, looking into Violet's eyes. Boss shoved Violet aside and tried to lick my hand through the wire.

For some weird reason, before I even knew I was crying, I felt big cool tears on my cheeks. Violet's sad eyes looked sadder than ever. "It'll be okay," I told her, reaching to rub my finger on her wet leathery nose. I suppose that sometimes the other two dogs really know Violet is my favorite.

Just then I heard a car coming up our lane. At the same second Pirate and Boss heard it, too, and barked their way to the end of the run. But Violet stayed at the side fence as if she knew I was in trouble and did not want to desert me.

I stood up and looked toward the Alcott house. It was a police car! I dropped back down into the grass. What should I do? They must be coming after Pesha. Scared as I was, I had to know exactly what was going on up at that house.

Between me and the Alcott house there was the summer pagoda, and then to the left and closer still to the house was the big live oak and a clump of scrub pine. Just as the police car stopped in the circle drive at Mrs. Alcott's back door, I reached the pagoda. The slatted sides were completely covered with gnarled wisteria vines that hid me.

Only one of the two policemen got out of the car. The second one stayed in the driver's seat. His head was turned away from me. I made a short dash across to the big oak. I was sure I could hear everything that was said from there.

I tried to swallow, but my mouth was too dry. I heard something that sounded like a hurt animal from inside the house. The back door opened and Pesha and Mrs. Alcott appeared. Even from where I was I could see that Pesha was scared to death. Mrs. Alcott was saying, "It's only for questioning. Please — do you want me to go with you?"

How could Mrs. Alcott say that if Leedie Ann really was inside? Would she leave Leedie Ann there alone? Had Mrs. Alcott really lost her mind like Sarah's mom said might happen?

"We can't take you along in the patrol car," the policeman said, "but you can follow, ma'am." His voice was rough with feeling sorry for Pesha, I suppose. But maybe not, because then he grabbed Pesha by the wrist and pulled her away from the doorway. Pesha fell. Her knees just seemed to give way with her the way mine felt like they might do any minute.

The policeman scooped Pesha back up to her feet. She was hitting at him like she was fighting for her life. I felt sorry for her even if she was a Gypsy and put spells on people.

Then Mrs. Alcott was begging again. "Pesha, you'll be back here in a few hours. Don't be so frightened." But now even Mrs. Alcott's voice sounded doubtful as the policeman pulled Pesha along. She looked back over her shoulder, silently now, as if she was begging Mrs. Alcott to do something.

Just for the flash of a second before the policeman got Pesha into the car, she turned her head and looked in my direction. Her eyes were wild with fear. I jumped behind the tree and made myself as little as possible. Had she seen me watching them? Would she put a curse on me?

Long after the police car had disappeared down our lane, and Mrs. Alcott had vanished back inside the big stone mansion, I stood clinging to the rough bark of the old tree. This wasn't working out at all the way I had planned.

8

Soon as I figured it was safe, I slowly retraced my steps back down toward the kennels. On the way, I glanced toward our house, but there was no sign of life. Apparently Dad was still deep into his work.

The dogs were as glad to see me as if I'd been away for a week instead of a few minutes.

I dropped down in the grass again and just bawled like a baby. I was in a terrible mess. I've been in trouble before, but it was always the kind of trouble where I could say I was sorry and that I wouldn't do that again. Worst of all I didn't dare tell anyone — certainly not Dad — that I had written that letter.

I desperately needed to talk to Sarah. She'd say it was all my fault, of course. And it was. But I needed to get her promise that she wouldn't confess to her mother what *I* had done and what *she* had a part in doing.

I wiped my face with my palms and dried my hands on my jeans. Pirate and Boss had laid belly down onto the cool earth. But Violet was on her haunches looking at me in a questioning sort of way. I stuck my hand through the fence and rubbed her under her chin, which she loves. She raised her chin and then licked my hand, probably tasting my salty tears. I took a deep breath. "Good dogs," I said and looked up toward the big house.

What were Mrs. Alcott and Leedie doing right this second? It all seemed too crazy and mixed-up.

I told the dogs good-bye and headed for home. On the way I glanced up toward Leedie Ann's bedroom. The curtains were still closed. Was she really in there? Or had Sarah and I both just imagined we saw her? How could we both have imagined it? The main thing was that I had to talk to Sarah, and I had to do it right away.

Dad looked up from his desk as I came through the doorway. "They picked up the Gypsy woman," he said, leaning back in his chair and rubbing his forehead. "There was a big commotion."

"I heard it," I admitted. "I was — down at the kennel."

Then I did, at last, get a lucky break. Dad said, "I have to run into town to the courthouse to check on a couple of dates. I want you to ride along, Kiley. With all this going on I need to know where you are."

It was kind of a nice feeling to have Dad worrying about me. Maybe if worse came to worst he could keep them from putting me in jail.

"Could you let me off at Sarah's and then pick me up?" I asked, crossing my fingers inside my jeans pocket.

"Okay," he agreed in a voice I knew meant he'd probably even forgotten what he was saying okay about.

Sarah's mom met me at the door with bad news. "Sarah isn't here, Kiley," she said, looking almost glad to tell me that. "What did you want?"

"Just to talk to her," I said with a sinking sort of feeling.

"Well, she isn't here," Mrs. Brock said. Did she already know about the letter to Pesha? "Where is she?" I blurted out. I felt as if I'd better stick my foot in the door to keep her from closing it.

Mrs. Brock sighed. "She was invited to Linda Ricy's house for lunch," she said, and this time she did close the door.

Linda Ricy lived only a couple of blocks away. I decided to take a chance on missing Dad because it was so important that I talk to Sarah.

I wondered why Linda had invited Sarah to lunch. They weren't even friends. Linda was in with the popular group in our class. I knew that the feeling inside me was part worry about the letter and part jealousy. I had a pit-of-the-stom-ach rushing need to talk to Sarah — to make sure of our friendship. I also needed to be sure she would keep our secret about the letter as we had agreed.

Linda lives in a big house with a circular drive. Soon as I started up the drive I saw the two of them, Linda and Sarah, sitting on the wide front porch in high-backed wicker chairs. They were drinking Cokes.

"What do you want, Kiley?" Linda asked just like Sarah's mom had.

"I need to talk to Sarah," I said, bossy as I could. "Alone," I added. I was still standing at the bottom of the steps. "Okay, Sarah?"

Sarah stood up, but Linda pulled at her shirt to sit back down. "Since she's my company, I should hear, too," Linda said.

"No way," I said firmly. "Sarah, *please*."

Sarah glanced first at Linda, but she got up again and came down the steps.

We walked a little way back down the drive. "The police have our letter," I whispered as soon as we were safely out of Linda's hearing.

Sarah gave her wrists a little shake. "I know!" she said desperately. "Kiley, what are we going to do?"

"Absolutely nothing," I said touching her shoulder. "You've got to promise you won't tell one soul. Sarah, we *could* be arrested—like Pesha. Promise!"

Sarah nodded and turned to go back with Linda. I grabbed her hand to stop her. "Out loud," I said.

"I promise, Kiley," she said and pulled her hand lose. She turned away again.

"Best friends?" I called after her not even caring that Linda was probably listening to me beg.

Sarah turned again and took a couple of steps back toward me. "My mother says that until all this is settled — about Gypsies and kidnapping — I can't come out to your place. And she even wishes — well, we'd stay apart a while, Kiley. Kiley, I'm sorry." Sarah had tears in her eyes this time when she turned to go back up to the porch.

I started slowly back toward her house to wait for Dad to come pick me up. I felt like a stray dog nobody wants around.

9

When I got to Sarah's house I sat down on the curb to wait. Dad came along right away.

"What's the matter, Kiley Mulligan?" he asked, surprised I guess that I was out front.

"Sarah isn't home," I said truthfully enough.

"Too bad," Dad said, "you've had a long wait. I was longer than I thought."

I didn't answer. Dad went on talking, "I heard at the courthouse they've taken Pesha back to Mrs. Alcott's. Didn't book her. But they're sure to get a warrant and pick her up again. We haven't gotten to the truth of the whole business, yet."

I sneaked a sideways look at him. It was as if he was warning *me*. I almost blurted out the whole awful story, but I clamped my teeth together and

kept quiet. All I could do was pray *somebody* would
discover that Leedie was safe at home and this
whole thing about the letter would be forgotten.

The next two days were the worst days of my
life. I missed Sarah something awful. I even wished
school was still going on so I could at least see
her. I spent a lot of time down at the kennels.
That's where I was when the dogs' barking warned
me again that a strange car was coming up our
drive.

It was another police car with two men in the
front seat. I sneaked up behind the live oak the
same as before to listen. I had to know what was
going on — no matter how bad it was. As I watched
both men get out of the car and head toward Mrs.
Alcott's back door, my heart twisted for Pesha.
Maybe this time she won't be so scared, I tried
to tell myself.

This time did turn out to be different. Mrs. Alcott came to the door alone. I couldn't hear what
they were saying until Mrs. Alcott said in a louder,
almost angry voice, "I've told you all I know. She
left in the night. I do *not* know where she's gone."

Pretty soon the policemen got back in the car

and drove slowly down our lane looking to the right and to the left as if they were searching for someone — Pesha, of course.

Pesha must have run away! I couldn't help but be glad. I didn't think I could stand to see her frightened eyes when the police came again. I guess it was knowing I had caused all her trouble that was making me feel that way.

After Mrs. Alcott closed the back door, I looked once more up toward Leedie's bedroom. This time the curtains were open, but it being daylight I couldn't see inside. I did think I saw a shadow move behind the windowpane, but I couldn't be positive sure. Was it Leedie, or was Pesha hiding up there?

I wandered on back to our house. Dad was just putting the cover on his typewriter. "Have to make a trip into town again today, Kiley Mulligan," he said. "You'll have to ride along."

I knew I couldn't go to Sarah's house, so I said, "This is the day Old Terry cleans the kennels. He likes me to help."

"Well, remember you're not to go wandering far," Dad said and picked up a fat manila envelope which meant he was going to the post office.

After Dad left I started back to the kennels to wait for Old Terry. The dogs are always kept locked in and only Mrs. Alcott and Old Terry have keys. But Old Terry is always glad to let me come inside and help him. With school going on I hadn't had much chance to help him lately.

I was walking along slowly with my head down thinking about Sarah being friends with popular, but spoiled, Linda. I kicked at a clump of feathery-leafed sea oats. Suddenly I stopped dead still. I backed up a step. Sure enough! There, shining under the edge of the clump, was a golden coin. I picked it up. The words on it were strange to me. The coin had a tiny hole in one edge as if it had been on a chain. Pesha! Pesha wore a chain with golden coins hanging from it around her ankle. But Pesha never came down toward the kennels — unless . . .

I looked around feeling shivery even though it was a sunny day. If the coin really did fall off Pesha's ankle chain, and if Pesha had run this way last night in the darkness, she would have been heading for the swamps. Nobody would go in there. Or maybe . . . I looked way past the kennels to the quarters where slaves had lived long ago. Could

Pesha be hiding in one of those little crumbly brick buildings?

The five little houses huddle together in one straight line. Above the row of them, witches' hair moss hangs off the skinny branches of a few old, dead trees. The whole place seems to be haunted with ghosts of people who were miserable because they were not free. I'd only been down there once. That was when we first moved here. But that was enough. Not that I was scared really. But it was such a sad alone place.

I pictured the inside of the buildings smothered in spiderwebs. Even birds that fly accidentally into a window or door space always fly right back out. Inside each one-room building is a big stone fireplace that swallows up most of the only un-broken wall.

How could anyone think they could hide in there for very long? Still, I had to know. My feet kept moving me along until I crossed the sandy field and came to the first doorway.

There are no steps. I stayed on the ground and peeked slowly inside.

Pesha was in there! I pressed my knees to-gether to stop their shaking. She was huddled into one corner like a heap of red and yellow clothes with no bones inside them to make a shape. For an awful second she just sat there and stared at me with smouldering black eyes.

Then she sprang up so fast that I took a little step backward.

"No!" she whispered in a hoarse voice. "Don't go! Quickly, child! Here inside! You must help me." She held out her hands palms up and crooked her fingers motioning me to come in.

I glanced back across the field toward the kennels. Old Terry was nowhere in sight to hear me if I screamed.

I looked again at Pesha. Her dark eyes seemed to hypnotize me. I took the high step up to the cement floor inside the slave quarters.

Pesha had on a wrinkled red skirt and yellow flowered blouse. Her brown feet were bare, but around her ankle was the gold chain with the coins.

"Is this yours?" I asked her, holding out the coin I had found. I was stalling to think what I should do. How did she mean "help" her? If I helped her when the law was after her, would that make me guilty of one more thing? I was sure I knew the answer. But if I helped her, maybe I

61

could find out the answer to why Leedie Ann was being kept secretly inside her own house.

Pesha reached for the coin. Her hands and arms were as brown as the inside skin on a hazelnut. "Yes, it is mine," she said. "Now you got to help me. The police. I didn't do nothing wrong. You must bring me food so I can hide. You must tell no one." She grasped my wrist which was still sticking out toward her holding the coin.

As I hesitated, wishing she'd let go of my wrist, she added in a pleading voice, "If you help me I will make a *diwano* for you."

"A *diwano*?" I asked, dropping the coin to the floor and pulling my wrist away. I wasn't sure but figured anything she might do could put a Gypsy spell on me. "What's that?"

"A *diwano* to bring you health and money and many friends," she answered.

I thought about Sarah. "Could you make a *diwano* to get me back a friend I lost?" I asked. "And to make her mom like me?" I added quickly.

Pesha's eyes turned to narrow slits. She looked even more mysterious as she cocked her head as if she was listening to a far-away voice. "I can do that," she promised at last.

It was hard not to believe her — about the *di-wano* getting me back my friend Sarah. And after all I *did* write the letter that got her into this trouble. Still —

"Please," Pesha said as if she had read my mind. "I'd like your understanding. I don't know nothing about the letter the police have. You will not be sorry." She touched my arm and the gold rings on her fingers felt cold. There was a spicy smell about her that seemed to come from the tiny cloth drawstring bag tied around her throat.

"Okay," I said. "But I'll have to get the food right away — quick — before my dad comes back from town. He'd be sure to tell the sheriff if he knew where you were."

A shadow crossed Pesha's face at the mention of the word sheriff. "Then go!" she said, giving me a little shove.

10

I jumped to the ground and ran toward our house. This time as I ran past the kennel, the dogs barked in a businesslike way as if they were glad I had at last discovered there was something strange going on around their territory.

"Right back, fellas," I called, hurrying on past. I raced inside our house and straight to our cubby-hole of a kitchen. Dad is very particular about the kitchen, and I reminded myself to leave everything as neat as it was.

My hand was shaking as I opened the refrigerator. There was a big bowl of black-eyed peas. A few spoonfuls would never be missed. I dumped them into one of the little margarine tubs Dad saves under the sink to store leftovers in. Next I cut off a slice of leftover meatloaf — not too thick or Dad might notice. Bread was safe. She'd have to eat it without butter because I didn't dare take that much more time. I grabbed up a handful of chocolate-chip cookies which I snack on all the time anyway, so they'd never be missed.

I dug a spoon out of the silverware drawer and crammed everything into one of the grocery sacks Dad folds neatly and saves in a drawer. . . .

I stopped before I went out the front door to listen for the sound of Dad's pickup. Nothing. Outside I looked around cautiously. The coast was clear — unless someone was secretly watching out the window of the big house. I had to chance that. I was sure that even if Old Terry was at the kennels now, he'd be too busy to notice me. He wasn't anywhere in sight as I ran past the kennels and straight to the old slave quarters.

Once I got safely inside, I took a deep breath. Pesha was sitting on the floor again with her back against the wall. She stood up and reached for my bag.

"You are a good person — for a *gorgio*," she said. "You've never known hunger." It wasn't a question, so I didn't answer.

Instead I said right out, "Why are you scared

to talk to the police? You really *do* know where Leedie Ann is. I have proof."

She reached the arm she wasn't eating with toward me as if to stop what I was going to say. "No," she whispered. "I came here to help out — to find the small one through my seances. I have not found her. We Gypsies are blessed with a deep insight — a *seeing*. I thought Mrs. Alcott would tell me more than she knows. I listen. But — " Pesha spread her hands palms up which I took to mean "but nothing happened."

She was lying of course. Leedie Ann *was* home! I had seen her. Sarah had seen her.

I guess having all that special sight she could tell I didn't believe her, which I didn't, because she said, "I am a seer. Not a person who steals children."

"I didn't say you stole her. I said she's home now . . . there . . . inside the big house."

"No. You are wrong."

"I saw her. I saw her in the window of her very own bedroom!"

"You saw a shadow," Pesha said softly. "Your mind lied to you." She sounded like my father, but I had more proof.

"My friend Sarah was right inside Mrs. Alcott's house and saw Leedie," I said.

"The mind imagines many things."

"No, it's true," I said trying to remember to keep my voice down. "She was in her bedroom. Just standing there. A couple of days ago."

"Standing?" Pesha looked toward the ceiling as if trying to get a vision of what I had described. "Beside the window?"

Then she looked deep into my eyes again. "Oh, *gorgio* child. It was not the little girl. When Mrs. Alcott has the store to sell children's clothing, she brought home the large-as-life doll-child. The mannequin she calls it. She has told me that before the little one was stolen away, she begged for this doll big as herself. So the mother brought it home and put it there for when the child returns. You saw the *figure* made of earth."

I almost started bawling. I believed her. Leedie Ann was not home and safe. I could believe now that what I had seen was only a mannequin from Mrs. Alcott's store. Leedie would never have stood so still. I had caused all this awful trouble for nothing. My head was spinning my thoughts around.

"You will not tell I am here?" Pesha pleaded.

I shook my head. It was the least I could do now to help make right all the wrong things I had done. But the warm happy feeling that had been deep inside me since the night I first thought I saw Leedie, my little pretend sister, standing in her bedroom window, had left me. The place that feeling had filled was empty and scared.

"I have to go," I said, ashamed to even look at Pesha's poor haunted face. "My dad — " Now I really was crying. Leedie Ann was gone for good and always.

"But tomorrow you will bring more food?" Pesha whispered, grabbing hold of my hand.

I looked around. Pesha was brave enough to stay all night here in this ugly place — alone — like a hunted small fox. And all because of me. "I'll come tomorrow," I promised.

11

I didn't even feel like stopping to help Old Terry anymore. Halfway to our house I stopped beside one lone loblolly pine and looked up at Leedie's window. I had to keep telling myself, Leedie is not safe at home. That was only a mannequin I saw standing like a hollow ghost-doll waiting, watching with painted-on eyes for little Leedie Ann to come play with her. My heart ached clear up to my throat. I knew that my life was ruined forever.

If only Sarah was still my friend. I couldn't talk to Dad. I'd be sure to blurt out something about the letter.

What would Dad do if he knew I wrote it? Would he just give me a lecture? No. This time the trouble I caused went too deep. The police — the whole town was a part of it. I would have to keep the letter a secret until the day I died.

Dad's pickup pulled up our lane just as I reached the front door. I hated to face him for fear he might guess how scared and worried I was. I certainly knew that Sarah's mom would have been able to tell that something terrible was wrong if she had laid eyes on me.

I was almost sure Sarah hadn't told her mom our secret, yet, or everyone in town would know. Dad would know.

As he got out of the car he called, "Hi, Kiley Mulligan," and reached into the cab of the truck for the sacks of supplies. "What are you up to?"

I could tell by his voice he didn't expect an answer. "Need me to help?" I asked casually as I could.

He held two large grocery sacks. "This is it." Then as I opened the door for him he said, "The town's on a Gypsy hunt. Everyone's convinced that a Gypsy tribe is holding Leedie Ann Alcott captive. That letter has stirred the whole sorry mess up again. It's as if the kidnapping happened yesterday." Dad sighed. "But maybe some good will come of it."

I eased the door closed and rubbed my sweaty palms down my jeans legs. What if Dad noticed the missing food when he put the groceries away? I'd have to say I ate it myself. He'd never believe me because of the black-eyed peas.

"But Dad," I said as I followed him into the kitchen, "Pesha already told the police she didn't have anything to do with all this."

"She ran away, Kiley," Dad said with his head in the refrigerator. "Of course she knows something. We're all hopeful now that she does. But I don't know. I do know that Gypsies wouldn't harm that child. Pesha knows something. That's why she ran."

"She ran 'cause she's scared of the police!" I blurted out before I thought.

Dad turned and looked at me for a second. But all he said was, "No use your getting upset about this, Kiley. That won't set things to rights."

I went into my bedroom and sat on the floor by the window. My window faces Crescent Cross Road and beyond that there's the ocean. I thought about asking if I could ride my bike down to Undertow Beach where Sarah and I used to go. But I really knew there was no use asking. Dad had said I was to stick around close and that meant staying here on the Alcott property. Around the house, the kennels, or even the old slave quarters.

The quarters — where the very person the whole town of Meander was searching for was hidden. I wasn't scared of Pesha anymore. I thought, maybe even if people are different from you, you aren't scared of them if you know them — know they are good. Maybe you even begin to feel sorry for them — the way I felt about Pesha.

I felt those same great cool tears on my cheeks that hadn't even seemed to come out of my eyes the way normal hot tears do.

I thought about Sarah. Did she miss me with the same ache I missed her? Probably not. She had a new friend now. A friend who wouldn't get her into trouble the way I did.

To get my mind off all this, I reached for my library book, *Stranger in White*. Our librarian saves me the new mystery books to read, then she always asks what I thought of them. This book was really good, and I had been trying to keep myself from reading it too fast because I hated to get to the end of it. But when I tried to read, all I could think about was Leedie Ann and Pesha.

The next morning I woke up already worrying about how I was going to get Pesha's food out of the house if Dad stayed home all day. I lay there thinking hard as I could and finally came up with a great plan.

At about eleven o'clock I told Dad I thought I would pack me up a picnic lunch and go outdoors to eat.

"Sounds great," he said, looking up from his typewriter. He rubbed his forehead. "Sounds so good I could almost join you."

Powie! There went my plan. But then Dad rubbed his chin as he looked at the stack of papers on the left side of his desk. He thumbed through them. "Better not," he said shaking his head. "Mind making me a sandwich to eat here at the desk? And don't go off the place."

I breathed again. "If you're hungry as I am you could eat three or four sandwiches," I lied. I wasn't even one drop hungry, but I wanted to get by with packing up lots of food for Pesha.

A little later I put Dad's baloney sandwich and a glass of milk on his desk and left.

For once I was glad he was too deep into his work to think about me.

12

Pesha was waiting propped up in one corner with her head on her knees. I cleared my throat so she would know it was me. She jerked her head up, looking so startled that I figured she'd maybe been asleep.

"I brought your food," I said. "And mine, too. We'll sort of have a picnic, okay?"

"Yes," she said. "You are good." I split the grocery sack open out flat like a cloth and spread out the food. Pesha gave me a little questioning look and reached for a sandwich and began eating.

I saw that she had letters tattooed on her right arm, but I couldn't tell what they spelled. Neither of us said anything while she ate the sandwich then took one of the apples and half of the cookies and stuffed them into the huge pocket in her red

74

skirt. I picked around at my food, but I still wasn't one bit hungry.

Dad always makes us a big breakfast and that morning it had been grits and eggs with hot biscuits made out of one of those cans that when you open the can the biscuit dough pops out at you. I figured I would leave the rest of my food here for Pesha in case I couldn't come back tomorrow.

"You didn't tell I was hiding here?" Pesha said.

"I didn't tell," I assured her. It seemed awful to me that here she was, a grown-up, hiding away from the police in the old slave quarters. She had nothing to sleep on, or cover up with if the nights got cold. How long could she stay here like this? "Don't you have any family? Any kids?" I asked her.

"I belong to a large family — the Kalderasha," she said. "I am married to Pepe since I was fifteen."

"Is Pepe the one who writes you letters sometimes?" I asked.

As soon as I said "letters" I knew that was a mistake. Pesha put her lips together tight like she was letting me know she had said all she was going to say. But after a minute she said, "I need to

trust you. You already know of the other letters — the ones before the bad letter that made
them hunt me?"

I nodded.

"Will you go each day and see if there is such
a letter there for me? Bring it here to me. With
the food. I will reward you."

I nodded again. After all, I was about as deep
in trouble as I could ever get. "Does Mrs. Alcott
know where you are — here, I mean?" I asked
her.

"Oh, no," Pesha said. "She is troubled enough.
I didn't come to her to make the *hokkani baro* —
the big haul. My dealings with her are *caco* —
on the up and up."

"But I don't understand," I said. "If you don't
know where Leedie Ann is — who kidnapped her,
why did you think you could help find her?"

Pesha's voice got mysteriously low. Her eyes
seemed to burn into mine. "We Gypsies have our
ways of knowing," she said. "On hot nights, when
the heavy moon hangs down, the spirits tell us
many secrets. We guard these secrets well and
use them only for good." She took hold of my
hands and this time her touch felt good. She was

76

talking to me as if I were another grown-up.

"Which is greater, the oak or the dandelion?" Pesha asked. And then she answered herself. "Whichever one achieves fulfillment." Her low voice was beautiful, like music in the wind off the ocean. "The Gypsy woman achieves fulfillment by using her gifts to help those in great trouble."

Suddenly she let go of my hands and jumped to her feet so fast her skirt swirled around her brown ankles. I stood up, too, feeling she was letting me know it was time to leave. But again she reached out and put one thin brown hand on each of my shoulders. "I'd like your understanding, child. You must believe that I am not a coward — hiding here like the animals of the wood and wold. For now I'd like your understanding. There are things — long ago with my people — my mother — in Germany. . . . There was a place — the picture of it never leaves my mind, the smell never leaves my senses, the hurt of it never leaves my heart. But go now! Before you are missed by your father, go."

I wasn't really worried that Dad would look for me, but I didn't say so. I picked up my book and checked to make sure there was no one in sight.

The coast was clear, so I jumped to the sandy ground. "I'll be back tomorrow," I promised.

Late that afternoon Dad began putting away his papers and closing his typewriter. "I have to go to the library, Kiley Mulligan," he said. "I wish you'd ride along with me. Maybe your friend will be home this time."

"No, I can't," I said before I thought. "I mean, sure, I'll go along, but — well, I want to go to the library, too. I finished my book." I hadn't finished my book, of course. Now I'd have to take a perfectly good mystery back without finishing it. I was too unhappy to read anyway.

To get to the library we had to drive right past Sarah's house. I looked but I didn't see any sign of her.

Our library isn't very big. It sits on a corner a block off Main Street. In the grass outside there is a big rock — maybe a boulder — with a bronze plate on it saying what year Mr. Carnegie gave the library to Meander.

I picked up the first book I came to and sat down at one of the long tables to pretend to read until Dad finished.

A couple of boys from my class, Jimmy Brown

and Al Broadman, came over to my table. Jimmy had a thick book from the adult side, and they sat down and opened it between them.

"Hey, Kiley," Jimmy said in a loud whisper. "Have they caught that Gypsy kidnapper out there on your place, yet?"

I felt my face get hot and knew they could tell that bothered me. I shook my head and pretended to go on reading.

Jimmy scooted over to the chair next to me. "I'll bet you know something you're not telling," he said in a low voice.

Inside I felt like screaming. He was too close to the truth. Except that, of course, Pesha was *not* a kidnapper. "Why don't you go back to your own chair and tend to your own business?" I whispered.

Al, who is a sort of dopey kid, picked up on that right away. He scooted over next to Jimmy and leaned across him. "Hey! She really does know something!"

I closed my book and shoved back my chair so loud that the librarian looked sternly in our direction and cleared her throat. I got up and went over to the reference section where Dad was copying off stuff from one of the books. I whispered that I would meet him at the car.

I stopped at the desk to check out the book I had picked up. Miss Thompson, our librarian, looked at me sort of funny and said, "Kiley, you read this book quite some time ago."

"But — I — I liked it," I said weakly.

"Have they caught that wild Gypsy out on your place yet?" Miss Thompson asked as she stamped the book.

For the first time in my life I felt like telling a grown-up to shut up. I realized in that split second that Pesha was my friend. She needed me. I said, "You know, Miss Thompson, it isn't really true that Gypsies steal children. They have plenty of their own, and their own children have Gypsy blood like they do. And Pesha isn't wild."

Miss Thompson looked as shocked as if I *had* said shut up. But she handed me my book and I went on outside to wait for Dad.

About noon the next day I told Dad that I was going to take my lunch down by the kennels again.

Dad gave me a questioning look. Then he stood up from his desk and stretched. For a breath-holding second I thought that this time he really was going to say he'd go with me. But instead he said, "I realize you feel pretty fenced in these days, Kiley Mulligan, and I'm sorry. They're bound to find the Gypsy woman soon — unless she's rejoined her own people heading north for the summer, which may make it harder to track her down."

He looked out the window toward the big house. "Yesterday the librarian told me that Mrs. Alcott is helping the police all she can, but she refuses to believe Pesha had anything to do with that letter. Mrs. Alcott told the police that Pesha is frightened because during World War Two when Pesha was a child" — Dad turned from the window and looked at me — "about your age, Kiley, her whole family was dragged off by the Nazis to Auschwitz. That was a concentration camp. Of all her family only Pesha survived. The rest died in the gas chambers."

"But that was a long time ago," I cried stupidly. It was stupid because I know that if your mother died it doesn't matter how long ago it was, it still hurts. And dead that awful way! Still I didn't want to believe that such a horrible thing had happened to Pesha.

"But in school," I insisted, "we learned it was

81

Jews who the Nazis killed in concentration camps."
Maybe Pesha had lied to Mrs. Alcott. I hoped so
with all my heart.

"Kiley," Dad said, looking sad, "almost one million Gypsies from Hungary, Romania — all over
Europe — were also rounded up during the war
and put to death in gas chambers." Dad shook his
head as if he wished he could shake out that awful
thought.

I pictured a long-ago Pesha, just a kid, alone
and terrified, in a concentration camp with sol-
diers. No wonder she was so scared of the police.
"If Pesha was in a concentration camp, how did
she get to this country?" I wondered out loud.

Still looking sad, my father ran one finger down
my cheek. "The Gypsies we see around Meander,"
he said, "claim to be from the Kalderasha tribe.
The ones who survived the concentration camps
in Germany applied for French citizens' papers.
Claimed theirs were lost in the war. Times were
so unsettled there was no way to prove this wasn't
true. From France they more or less legally en-
tered the United States." Then Dad smiled. "Run
along, honey," he said. "Have your picnic."

I touched the spot where his finger had traced

a line. Right then I almost confessed I wrote the letter that caused all the trouble. But I couldn't do it. I knew then I'd *never* be able to. I would have this awful guilty feeling inside me until I died.

13

When I got to the quarters, Pesha was waiting for me as usual. Only this time my mind saw her in a different way. She was a part of the history we studied in school. I had never thought of a concentration camp happening to people alive now.

Pesha looked tired. She didn't eat much of the food I'd brought, either. But she carefully put all that was left back into the sack and laid it in the corner where she was usually sitting hunched when I got there.

"You are good," she said in her music-in-the-wind voice. Looking at her I knew that what she was trying to say was that she was my friend. Probably she was my only friend — now that I'd lost Sarah.

I thought about asking Pesha about the *diwano*

she had promised to make to get Sarah and me back the way we used to be — friends, best friends. But it didn't seem like the right time for that. Anyway, I didn't think even a person with psychic powers could change Sarah's mom's mind once it was made up.

"You are unhappy," Pesha said looking deep into my eyes. "You are sad about the friend you have lost. You are sad because you had believed that the small *gorgio* child, Leedie Ann, was safe at home. The little girl you made a doll for — from a clothespin."

Pesha really *must* have psychic powers, I thought! How else did she know all that?

She smiled into my eyes. "You see you have told me more than you know. But the doll — you have been kind to me — I will be *caco* with you. Mrs. Alcott talked to me about the clothespin doll. She told me about the child taking only the doll you made for her, when she was stolen away from her home."

"And I am sad for you, too, Pesha," I couldn't keep from saying. "My father told me about the concentration camp — about your moth—. About all your people."

Pesha crossed herself with her thin brown fingers. She turned away toward the dusty fireplace and stood gazing into it. Had I said too much? Was she angry?

But then she whirled back around again making the golden ankle bracelet give a tiny tinkling sound. She looked at the sack of food lying in the corner.

"There was never enough to eat," she said in a low angry voice. "But my brothers, they were allowed to bring their violins along. They played sometimes — the Gypsy music. From all over the Gypsies were brought — together they played our Gypsy music — and sometimes even I danced."

Then Pesha slowly collapsed onto the cement floor like an umbrella going down. I sat facing her. I was truly hypnotized now by her words, her voice, her eyes. I knew I would hear more.

"My mother, Medilla was her name, gave her small portions of food to me. Slowly I watched her and the others starve until they were no longer able to do the work the Nazis required. The sick ones — my mother was among the first to be — " Pesha buried her face in her ringed fingers.

"Don't!" I whispered.

She held out both arms toward me as if begging for my understanding as she had said so often. "We Gypsies — like birds we must have our freedom," she whispered, "or die."

At last I saw what the tattoo on her arm spelled. A-U-S-C-H-W-I-T-Z!

I felt those cool tears on my cheeks again. I didn't even bother to brush them away.

Pesha put her hand under my chin and forced me to look into her eyes. "*Gorgio* child, Kiley — if some day when you come to this place I am gone, I want you to remember something. A Gypsy never forgets a road she has traveled."

I gave a little shiver. I wasn't sure exactly what she meant, but I did know for sure now that she was telling me in her own way that we were friends forever — no matter what happened.

"Go now, my *gorgio* friend, little True Rye," Pesha said in a pleading voice.

I got up and left without saying another word. But I knew that Pesha knew I really cared about her.

14

That night I kept having dreams about concentration camps. I dreamed Leedie Ann, holding her little clothespin doll, was being held a prisoner in one. And then my dream switched and I was Leedie's mother and Mrs. Alcott was my mother and she was being put to death in the gas chamber.

The next morning I wandered around the house until Dad finally said, "Kiley Mulligan, I will be glad when this whole thing about the Gypsies blows over so you can be free to ride to the beach or into town to see your friends again. You are like a restless monkey. Truth is, I can't work with you pacing around that way."

"Maybe I'm just hungry," I said. "I'll fix our lunch if you don't mind eating kinda early."

"That's great, honey," he said and ducked his head back over the page he was reading.

Truth was, I was anxious to get back to the quarters and make sure Pesha was okay. When I had her food gathered together and into a paper sack, I hid it behind the trash bag underneath one side of the sink.

After I had cleaned up from lunch, and Dad had gone back to his work, I rescued Pesha's food and headed for the quarters.

On the way down the kennel dogs barked me a welcome as usual. That's why I didn't hear footsteps following me. Suddenly, from behind I felt a strong hand clamp onto my shoulder. I jumped so hard my sack of food flew into the air and spilled as it landed upside down.

It was Dad. "What's going on, Kiley?" he asked in a dangerously quiet voice as he stared at the spilled food.

"I — I," I began, but I was shaking so hard I couldn't get the words past my teeth.

"You've already eaten lunch. Have you been taking out food to Mrs. Alcott's dogs?" he asked, looking incredulous.

I almost lied and said yes, but there was an

orange lying right there in plain sight. Dogs don't eat oranges. I thought about saying I was still hungry, but before I got the chance Dad looked beyond the kennel to the slave quarters. The expression on his face made my knees go weak. "Kiley," he demanded, "what kind of trouble are you in? It's Pesha, isn't it? Isn't it, isn't it!"

"She's scared, Dad," I cried. "Scareder than you can imagine — of the police. I had to help her."

"Helping someone evade the law is not helping," Dad almost yelled. He grabbed hold of my arm. "Which one is she hiding in?"

I couldn't keep from looking at the first little building in the row.

"So that is it!" Dad said. Leaving the sack lying there he tightened his hold on my arm and almost dragged me along back toward our house. "You had better hope, young lady," he said as he stomped along with me trying to keep up, "you'd better hope she is still there when the police get here. I'll do what I can, but. . . ." We were almost to our front door.

Dad looked back over his shoulder toward the quarters and I did, too. There was no sign of Pesha.

I prayed she hadn't heard! I pictured her, huddled in the corner, her thin brown hands covering her dark eyes.

"Please don't call the police," I begged. "Just tell Mrs. Alcott where she is. Pesha isn't afraid of *her*. You know how the concentration camps — the war. Her mother."

Dad frowned until his dark eyebrows were one straight line. "What on earth are you babbling about?" he shouted. "I can't believe a thing you say anymore, Kiley. First it is that you've seen the poor little Alcott kid and now this!"

By this time I was bawling so hard I couldn't have explained about Pesha's terrible fear of the law even if Dad would have listened.

Dad went straight to the phone the minute we got inside. I tried to tell myself it was for the best that the police find Pesha. That somehow then this whole mess would get straightened out. But I knew this wasn't so. It would never be straightened out unless I admitted writing that letter. The very thought made my heart pound.

Dad's call took only a second. "Dan Culver here at the Alcott place," he said. "The Gypsy woman you're looking for, sir, is here on the place." There was a short pause and then, "Yes, I'll be here." Dad hung up.

He turned to me. "Kiley Mulligan Culver," he said sternly, "no matter what happens or what you are asked, you are to stay entirely out of this. Do you understand? You are just a kid. Stop trying to run the world."

"Dad, if you'd listen — " I began, but he stopped me right there with his raised palm like a corner policeman when the light is red.

To emphasize it, he added, "NO MORE!"

I went over and stood by the front window. There wasn't a soul in sight. Old Terry had been there earlier in the day to feed the dogs. Mrs. Alcott's car was gone from the carport so I supposed she'd gone to our little country store for groceries like she did sometimes.

I couldn't see much of the quarters from here. Just the corner end of the very last one of the five buildings. Beyond that the marsh grasses waved in the wind and I could hear the first faint wail of the evening whippoorwills. Was Pesha as sad as those whippoorwills sounded?

I thought of how she'd said, " . . . the picture of it never leaves my mind, the smell never leaves my senses, the hurt of it never leaves my heart." She was talking about the concentration camp, of course. My own heart ached for her.

15

In almost no time the police cars, two of them, came roaring up our drive. Dad went to meet them. As he went out the door he said, "You stay put!"

I couldn't have moved if he'd told me to. I was so scared it felt as if my feet were stuck in cement.

But I couldn't stop watching. From the window I could see the policemen jumping out of their cars to meet Dad. Dad pointed toward the slave quarters. The three policemen starting running in that direction. Dad came back toward our house.

He can't stand to watch, I thought bitterly. He knows it's wrong for those men to come and take Pesha away to jail when she's so scared.

Dad didn't say a word to me when he got inside. He went straight on into his own bedroom, and I could hear him rummaging around as if he were looking for something.

I stood there by the window in an agony of fear. My eyes were blurry and my head felt dizzy. I thought I was going to throw up, but still I couldn't keep from watching.

And then I saw all four coming back from way behind the kennels. Two policemen held Pesha by the arms. Her hair was hanging down almost covering her face. But she wasn't struggling this time. She was so limp they were almost carrying her.

I still stood there without moving as one policeman rushed on ahead and opened the front door of the patrol car. I heard the door slam as the driver got in. Another policeman lifted Pesha in between them. I couldn't see her anymore, she was so little, crowded in between those two big men.

"Bullies!" I screamed not even caring that Dad could hear. The cars circled and sped off down our lane.

Just then Dad came back into the living room, and I realized I had sunk down to my knees there at the window and that my face was soaked with tears.

I rubbed the tears away quick as I could when Dad said, "Kiley Mulligan, I think it is time we had a serious talk." His voice sounded almost forgiving.

I stood up and turned to face him. He'd pulled a chair out from the table, and he pointed at another chair for me to sit in.

I leaned my elbows on the table. "What about?" I asked as innocently as I could manage because, of course, I knew. My mind was swimming with ideas about what I could use for a reason for helping Pesha without giving away that I was the one who got her into all this trouble.

"You know what about," Dad said, looking me straight in the eye. "What I want to know is, why?"

"I like her," I said, "I — "

"You didn't even know her!" Dad interrupted. "Kiley, your habit of rescuing stray birds and animals in risky situations is one thing. But stray *people?* You knew where Pesha was hiding, and you should have come to me immediately. You interfered with the law. That's serious."

I began to feel angry inside. I wanted to hurt

him. I wanted to hurt him because he wasn't a mother. How could I talk to him? He'd never understand. Since he never tried to understand how I felt, I simply would keep still — not say another word.

I pressed my lips together and stared toward the window. My insides had turned to Jell-O, but I was not going to let him know that!

Dad jumped up from his chair so fast the chair almost tipped over, and I jumped as if he had hit me. "Talk to me!" he yelled.

I made my eyes go narrow and looked straight at him. "Why? You wouldn't listen. Or understand. Or take my side for once."

Dad sat back down with a big sigh. "Kiley Mulligan, am I such a bad father as all that?"

"You're pretty busy all the time, writing," I said, softening a little bit myself. That kind of talk made me feel better. It was steering away from what I had done.

"Granted," Dad said. "I am busy. I have to stay busy or go back to teaching so we can eat, Kiley." He pounded his fist into his open palm. "How am I ever going to explain this; your hiding that Gypsy woman, taking her food so she could evade the law? Don't you care anything about Mrs. Alcott and her terrible loss?"

That made me break up. All my disappointment about Leedie Ann not being safe after all, bunched into one tight knot in my throat. I began to cry again. I longed so much for somebody to understand. To tell me what I had done was okay. Sarah? Did she hate me, too? Did even Pesha maybe hate me because she thought now I had told where she was hiding?

Dad got up and came around behind my chair and gave my shoulder a squeeze.

"I'm sorry," I said between sobs.

"Okay," Dad said in a discouraging voice. "I just hope you've learned something. A kid cannot straighten out the whole world. You can't *wish* Leedie Ann back and then tell me you saw her. That doesn't make it true."

"Pesha was in a concentration camp!" I yelled. "They didn't give them any food. She danced, but her mother died."

"I'm sorry about that, honey," Dad said. "Millions of people died in concentration camps. I can't — you can't — make it right for them now.

Even that doesn't give Pesha the right to evade the law. Especially when a child's life may be at stake."

"Her mother was killed on purpose — with gas!" I screamed. "And I hate you!" I jumped up and ran into my bedroom, slamming my door as hard as I could.

16

During supper that night, and all the rest of the evening, Dad and I never mentioned what had happened. In fact we hardly talked at all. I kept my eyes on the TV even though I wasn't watching it. Dad read the stack of mail and newspapers that had come that week.

The next morning right after breakfast Dad said, "I'm going in to the library. Why don't you call your friend Sarah and ask her to meet you there?"

I could tell he was trying to be nice. But, I warned myself, he wouldn't be being nice if he knew the whole truth. Meet Sarah? That sounded great to me. But would she come?

I gathered my courage and dialed Sarah's number while Dad was shaving. Even though our house is small, he wouldn't be able to hear over the sound of his electric razor if I was careful and talked quietly.

Sarah's brother Adam answered! He'd be sure to say, "Oh, hello, *Riley*," and then Sarah's mom would know it was me. So I disguised my voice as much as I could to sound like Linda Ricy's drawl.

"This is Linda," I said with my heart beating clear up to my head. "Ah want t'talk to Sarah, please."

"About what?" Adam said mimicking my drawl.

I blew it then. "Please hurry, Adam," I begged in my own voice.

"Oh, it's you, kid," Adam said. "Just a minute Riley, my girl. I'll fetch her."

I almost fainted. I sure hadn't expected any favors from Adam. Maybe all those times I had laughed at his dumb jokes were paying off.

In just a second Sarah answered. "Hello, Kiley?" she said in a cool voice like she'd grown up since I saw her last and didn't really want to talk to a mere child.

"Meet me at the library, Sarah," I demanded. "I mean it. I'll be there in a half hour." I hung up before she could say no.

Would she come? When I hung up the phone, my hand left shiny sweat marks on the black plastic.

Sarah wasn't inside the library when Dad and I got there. Maybe her mom found out! I had a sinking feeling in my backbone that made me hunch over and hug my arms tight around my waist.

I went outside to sit on the library steps. Right away I saw her coming along the sidewalk toward the library. I almost ran to meet her; I was so glad. But I stayed where I was.

Sarah looked different. She had on some shorts with a matching top I'd never seen, and her curly hair went back off her face in little wings like it had been blown dry. But she's still the old Sarah inside, I reminded myself.

"I came as soon as I could," Sarah said, and I felt happiness wash away a little edge of my troubles. That was more like the old Sarah.

"I was scared your mom might have found out you were meeting me," I admitted.

Sarah looked at me kind of funny. "If she had, I wouldn't be here," she said.

"I suppose she's upset like the rest of the people

in this town about Gypsies stealing children," I said.

"No, it's worse than that," Sarah said and her cheeks turned pink. "She knows about the letter — the one we wrote. The one *you* wrote, but I sorta helped with."

This was the worst news Sarah could have told me. "How — how — ?" I couldn't go on. I pulled Sarah down to the steps so we could whisper.

"I told her," she said almost defiantly. She *had* changed after all. "And I got in plenty of trouble!" Sarah burst into tears, and I saw this new Sarah was only an act. "Oh, Kiley," she said, dabbing her tears with a folded tissue, "my mother made me promise I'd never even talk to you again!"

"But Sarah," I said, touching her arm to let her know it was okay about her mom. "If she knows about the letter, then everyone knows — or will!" My heart wasn't beating at all now!

"No," Sarah said, refolding her tissue and stuffing it into her shorts pocket. "She isn't going to tell. She made me promise I wouldn't tell one soul that I knew *anything* about the letter."

"I don't understand," I said.

Sarah sort of shook her head. "Well," she whispered, "my mother said it wouldn't be wrong for us to simply keep it quiet about the letter to Pesha until all this blows over. Then the letter won't be important. You see?"

Sarah sounded almost as if she was apologizing for her mom. There was a little silence and then she said, "Mother says I should stay completely out of this whole grown-ups' affair. That's okay isn't it, since Leedie really *is* safe in her own house?"

"Sarah," I began, "Leedie isn't — " Then I stopped. If I told Sarah that Leedie Ann wasn't home after all, she'd tell her mom, and her mom might think that made a difference in whether she let people know who wrote the letter or not.

"Never mind," I said. I didn't blame Sarah for telling. If I had a mother, I probably would have told her the whole story by now. Sarah's mom was keeping still about something important just to protect Sarah. Moms were probably like that. I knew from experience that dads weren't. I couldn't even think about what would happen if Dad knew I wrote that letter. I knew for sure he would have told. But for some reason thinking this made me feel proud of my dad.

"It's okay," I said. I couldn't stand for her to be unhappy, too. Just because my life was ruined.

Dad came out the library door just then. He had a stack of books under one arm. "Hi, Sarah," he said, "glad to see you. You've been a stranger lately. Can we give you a lift home?"

Sarah looked startled. I knew, of course, what was wrong. Her mother would see her with us. But it is almost impossible for Sarah to tell a lie. "I guess not," she said not looking at Dad. "I'd better not because — "

Sarah was my friend. I rescued her. "She has some errands, Dad," I said. "Come on. Let's go."

Dad gave me a look that said, I'll never understand kids, and started on down the steps ahead of us.

"Don't worry, Sarah," I said, and followed him.

Dad stopped the car at the post office, and I waited for him. When he came out he said, "The hearing for the Gypsy woman has been set for tomorrow."

Hearing? What would happen to her then? She was already so frail and thin, so scared of the law. She would never understand what was going on.

My heart felt as heavy as a balloon filled with water.

All the rest of that day I couldn't get Pesha off my mind. Nor Sarah. She *did* miss me, I could tell. And she wasn't going to be best friends with Linda. She was, or at least I figured she was, feeling as mixed up about things as I was. The truth about the letter sat like a stack of heavy books on my mind.

Late that afternoon the phone rang. I was so edgy I jumped. Dad answered it. I listened as he said, "All right. Yes, we will both be there. Two o'clock."

Both be there! Where? Why? As Dad hung up I looked quickly back at my book, pretending to read. But the words were a blur.

"They want us both at the hearing, Kiley," Dad said.

I finally got out one word. "Why?"

"Because we live out here, of course," Dad said with a tired sigh. I supposed the sigh was because of me. His own daughter standing in the way of "the law," as they say in the western shows.

I *wanted* to tell him there was even more. I longed like a toothache to tell him there was worse.

But I didn't dare. He was sure to report that to the police, too. I'd probably go to jail the way Pesha had.

"I'm sorta worried about Violet," I said, to change the subject. "She isn't acting like herself lately. She's sorta droopy. Even Old Terry noticed," I added for good measure. It was really a lie — the part about Old Terry noticing. But Violet knew I was unhappy, and her eyes had been looking sadder than ever.

"Please don't try to play vet and doctor her," Dad warned. "That would be about what you'd be up to. Some things are better left to adults — who know what they are doing."

I tried to hang onto that. I *could* just leave this whole terrible mess to adults. But somehow that didn't seem to make me feel more comfortable.

17

The next afternoon the time to leave for Pesha's hearing came fast, the way things you dread always do.

Dad and I started out early because as Dad said, the whole town would crowd into the courthouse. As we drove up and parked, we could see he was right. There were people milling all around the front of the old brick building.

When we got to the courtroom where the hearing was to be held, there was a guard at the door. They weren't letting any more people in because the room was almost filled. For a second I hoped he wouldn't let us in. But when the guard, who was Clemmet Watkins, saw it was Dad and me, he motioned us on through the door and toward two empty seats down near the front.

As we walked toward them, I tried not to look around at what seemed like a million people packed into the room. Where was Pesha? Would she have on handcuffs? Would she see me? Did she think I had betrayed her?

Then I saw Mrs. Alcott sitting a couple of rows ahead of our seats. At least, even if Pesha thought I had betrayed her, Mrs. Alcott would be a friendly face. A little ways away from Mrs. Alcott was Mr. Alcott. He must have driven in just for the hearing.

As Dad and I squeezed past Mrs. Rawley, the postmistress, and another woman, I heard Mrs. Rawley say, "The Gypsies have that child just as sure as cotton blooms."

The other one said, "That Gypsy is guilty as sin."

"Guilty as sin. Guilty as sin." The words kept running through my mind in a sort of threatening voice. Like a spooky movie with a voice coming out of a thundercloud.

The next thing I knew they were bringing Pesha in through a door at the front of the room. All the fire and life seemed to be gone out of her. Even her beautiful dark eyes looked dull. I remembered what she'd said about Gypsies having to be free or they died.

Was Pesha dying? She looked like she was. Her face was pale, and her lips were puckered tight until they looked like they had been gathered by a string. Her hair was straggly around her shoulders. But she held her head high.

I cleared my throat to keep from crying and squeezed my eyes shut so I wouldn't have to look at Pesha anymore.

Then Tom McLean, the lawyer, began asking Pesha questions about the letter. He wasn't really even asking. He was yelling questions at her one after the other. He leaned right up to her face and shouted.

I wanted to yell, "Stop! She didn't do it!" I pressed my knuckles hard against my mouth.

Suddenly the lawyer stopped yelling. A murmur of voices like a breeze through the palmetto branches rippled across the room. I opened my eyes. Pesha's head had fallen back and her eyes were all whites. She *is* going to die! I thought. I saw Mrs. Alcott sort of raise her hand and then let it drop back into her lap again.

Then Mr. McLean, the lawyer, raised his arm

like he was going to hit Pesha. But instead he shouted, "Answer the question!"

Pesha looked at him with her long brown fingers together as if she was praying. "I — " she said and stopped.

For a flash of a second the rest of the people in the room disappeared. There was only Pesha and me and that awful man yelling at her. Then I was standing and yelling back at him, "She doesn't know! She doesn't know!"

I heard as if from a long ways away, the roomful of people gasp. Then the whispering began again. It got louder until it was a distant roar like the ocean in my ears.

I felt as if I was far above everyone else's head; as if I was an inflated person floating in the air, but attached to a string. The string turned out to be Dad trying to pull me back down into my seat.

I brushed his hand away. Dad stood up beside me and said, "I'm sorry, Sir," to the judge.

"No," Judge Fisher said from his high seat. "Let Kiley talk."

Then I heard my own voice say as calmly as if I had been reciting in school. "I wrote the letter to Pesha about Leedie Ann."

111

Every person in the courtroom, which was at least half the people in Meander, was staring at me standing there alone. But I wasn't scared anymore.

I looked at Pesha. The look on her face was enough to make me glad for what I had done. It was love mixed in with hope. Her pool-dark eyes held me in a tiny safe Gypsy spell.

Then I ran. Tromping on feet to get to the aisle, I ran down it fast as I could. I ran out the door of the courtroom, down the empty hall and out the wide front door of the courthouse.

18

Suddenly something made me stop dead still in the middle of the sidewalk. It seemed to be the spell that Pesha's eyes had put on me. What was I running from? I was running from the truth! My dad didn't run from the truth when he told the police about Pesha even though he knew I had been helping her evade the law. Then I knew what Pesha's spell had done. It had made me realize that my dad and me, we were honest people.

I turned to go back to face Judge Fisher. I would even face going to jail. It was right then, still standing there in the middle of the sidewalk that I saw it!

What I saw was lying in the back window of a long black Lincoln car parked in front of the courthouse. It was the clothespin doll I had made for Leedie Ann!

I edged closer to be sure I was right. Yes, it was made from the same tiny red flowered material I had picked out of her sewing basket. And the same silly-looking pants I pulled up where the clothespin split for legs. But Leedie Ann had that doll with her the day she was kidnapped.

An idea began to grow in my mind. I looked at the license plate on the car—it was an out-of-state plate. What if — ? Or was this another of what Dad calls my crazy ideas? I had to take a chance.

I took off for the wide front steps of the courthouse. Let me be right this time, I prayed.

I passed a few straggling people in the courthouse hall. They turned and stared as I ran past them.

Inside the room the people were standing and talking in loud voices as they headed for the door.

I pushed my way through the aisle and ran straight up to where Judge Fisher still stood on his little perch talking to Mr. McLean below him.

The chair where Pesha had sat was empty now. I was so out of breath I could hardly talk. "The doll — the one I made for Leedie from a clothespin — she had it with her — "

Judge Fisher frowned at me. I glanced back to the front row where Mr. Alcott had been sitting. He was standing now, talking to a man in a baseball cap.

"What is it this time, Kiley?" the judge asked. "I suggest you and I have a little talk in my chambers."

"No! Here!" I begged. Then I leaned closer so he could hear me above the commotion. "I think I know where Leedie is! The clothespin doll she had with her when she disappeared is in the back of Mr. Alcott's car!"

Judge Fisher looked at me for what seemed ages. Then he turned to his desk and banged on it with his gavel for silence the way they do in the movies. "Will Mr. and Mrs. Alcott please meet with me in my chambers immediately."

Suddenly it was even more like a movie. Mr. Alcott looked at the judge, then at me, and his eyes got wide. He shoved the man in the baseball cap aside and made a mad dash through the still crowded aisle, scattering people right and left as he bolted for the door.

Luckily the guard heard the judge, and he stopped Mr. Alcott as he tried to escape!

In all this confusion I felt my dad's arm around me. I heard him say, "My daughter isn't in any trouble, is she, Judge Fisher? Because I can assure you that her intentions — "

Judge Fisher waved Dad and me aside. He turned away to go through the narrow door of his chambers, and Mrs. Alcott followed him. As she passed me she gave me a little smile, but her lips were trembling so that it disappeared before it hardly came.

The guard was bringing Mr. Alcott back down the aisle.

Dad hugged me. "I'm proud of you, Kiley Mulligan," he said. "Even if you did make a mistake not coming to me at the start of all this."

Dad was proud of me! That was all that mattered right that second. I was about to say, "But I *did* try to tell you." Then I changed my mind. There was a lot to think about right that minute.

Maybe, just maybe, now they really were going to find Leedie Ann and bring her home. Maybe all this time she had been with her father!

And it happened! The next morning I saw Mrs. Alcott's car coming up our lane, and there beside her safe and sound sat Leedie Ann.

I yelled back into our house, "Dad! Dad! She's *really* here! Leedie is home!"

Dad rushed out and together we walked over to the portico of the big house to welcome them. Leedie jumped out her door the second the car stopped and came flying toward me. "I'm home, Kiley," she screamed. "I'm home!" She didn't even call me "Kiwee" anymore. And she was taller. But she still had the same little dimple in one cheek, and her blonde hair was still in two little braids.

I guess it was the happiest happening of my life!

Mrs. Alcott and Dad were smiling and talking. Mrs. Alcott said, "I think since Kiley here is our hero, she should hear the whole story, too."

Then she told us that Mr. Alcott had tried to run out of the courtroom when he saw me talking to the judge because he thought I had seen him the day he stole Leedie away.

Mr. Alcott had kept Leedie hidden at the farm home of his old aunt and uncle until the search parties gave up. Then he had moved to another city with her.

"Her father loves her the same as I do," Mrs. Alcott explained to me. "And he took good care of her. Still, to steal Leedie Ann when I had custody was wrong! What a horrible time he put me through. I might never have gotten her back if it weren't for you."

I promised to make Leedie a new clothespin doll and after a while Dad and I started walking back over to our place.

When we got inside, the phone was ringing. It was Sarah. "My mother says I can come out and spend the whole day tomorrow, Kiley, if you want me."

"Oh, I do! I do, Sarah," I said. "I'll be waiting by the yaupon bushes at the end of our lane." Maybe Pesha had made that *diwano* thing for me after all.

Pesha! In all this excitement I had forgotten her. She hadn't been in the car with Mrs. Alcott and Leedie. Surely she was free now. I hung up and ran all the way to Mrs. Alcott's back door. I was sure it would be okay to bother Mrs. Alcott now. But Mrs. Alcott hadn't seen Pesha again, either!

Pesha didn't come back to the Alcott plantation. Nobody knew where she disappeared to. I thought about how that day a long time ago she had suddenly appeared walking up our lane. Nobody knew then where she came *from*, either.

I thought a lot about all the things Pesha had told me. Things about Gypsies having to be free and all. And I remembered her saying, "A Gypsy never forgets a road she has traveled." I feel sure now Pesha meant that someday, when the Gypsies make camp once more in the piney woods behind Undertow Beach, she will come walking up our lane again.

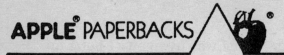